BILL
In A
CHINA
SHOP

For M&D, M&M, S, B&R, R, L.B.H.,
and of course, my editor, V.W.A. ~K.M.W.

For Bill & Lisa & Billy ~T.R.

There is some debate about the origin of the phrase "bull in a china shop."
One of the more interesting theories we've heard is this:
In the 17th century, Smithfield Cattle Market was established in London.
It is said that when the herdsmen drove their cattle through the streets to market
the beasts sometimes strayed into the nearby china shops.
Of course, we like to think that those bulls were made welcome by the shopkeepers...

BLOOMSBURY
CHILDREN'S
BOOKS

First published in Great Britain in 2003 by Bloomsbury Publishing Plc
38 Soho Square, London, W1D 3HB
This paperback edition first published in 2004

First published in America by Bloomsbury Children's Books USA, New York

Text copyright © 2003 Katie McAllaster Weaver
Illustrations copyright © 2003 Tim Raglin
The moral rights of the author and illustrator have been asserted

ISBN 0 7475 6491 4

Printed in China

10 9 8 7 6 5 4 3 2 1

All papers used by Bloomsbury Publishing are natural, recyclable products made
from wood grown in well-managed forests. The manufacturing processes conform
to the environmental regulations of the country of origin.

BILL In A CHINA SHOP

by Katie McAllaster Weaver

illustrated by Tim Raglin

BLOOMSBURY
CHILDREN'S
BOOKS

Once there was a bull named Bill
who felt a certain thrilling chill
each time he saw a china shop—

the teacups made his heart flip-flop.

He couldn't help but cry and pout

for each store's sign read, BULLS KEEP OUT.

But then one day he saw a store

without a sign upon its door.

So carefully he crept inside

and there upon a shelf he spied

a cup that made him want to shout,

a cup he could not live without.

Inching closer, almost to it,

one more step, but then he blew it.

His flailing tail flicked and whacked

a pile of platters, neatly stacked.

They leaned and lurched, then nearly tipped...

Whew! Back to normal, nothing chipped.

"Bulls are not allowed in here,"

the clerk said with a snarly sneer.

Aghast at what he nearly did,

Bill backed up, then tripped and slid

into a vase which broke in two,

which wasn't what he'd meant to do.

Frightened by the jarring sound

of china crashing to the ground,

he stumbled toward some figurines

and smashed them into smithereens.

"Bulls are not allowed in here,"

the clerk repeated with a sneer.

Looking like he just might cry,

Bill let out a heavy sigh.

Pointing to the cup he needed,

he groveled, begged, and even pleaded.

Full of fidgets and frustration,

giddy with anticipation,

Bill began to stomp and shake,

feeling like his heart would break.

Sugars, creamers, pots galore

exploded once they hit the floor.

Then three ladies tottered in; each one frowned from wig to chin.

"Oh, look at this untidiness. Mr. Bull, did you cause this?"

Bill nodded sadly, up and down,

as giant tears plopped to the ground.

"You poor, sweet dear," the ladies gushed,

for they could see that Bill was crushed.

Again the clerk said with a sneer,

"Bulls do not belong in here!

I'm sorry for this mess today.

This awful beast won't go away!"

The ladies patted poor Bill's head,

snarling at the clerk instead.

To the clerk they said, "How rude!"

Then to Bill they turned and cooed.

They bought his cup and also paid

for all the mess that Bill had made,

then packed the cup in tissue wrap

and tied it with a sturdy strap.

Beaming, Bill walked through the door

and thanked his friends outside the store.

When Bill the bull got home that day

he put his teacup on display.

Next he wrote his friends a letter:

Thanks to you I feel much better.

I hope you three will come to tea

so I can thank you properly.

Then one day at half past four

Bill heard knocking at his door.

His three friends all tottered in;

each one grinned from wig to chin.

"Here's to tea and bite-sized cakes;
here's to hoping nothing breaks!"